The Adventures of Jack and M

MILO MEETS A NEW FRIEND

Jennie Dial

Illustrated by Kathrine Gutkovskiy

LifeRich Publishing is a registered trademark of The Reader's Digest Association, Inc.

LifeRich Publishing books may be ordered through booksellers or by contacting:

LifeRich Publishing
1663 Liberty Drive
Bloomington, IN 47403
www.liferichpublishing.com
844-686-9607

ISBN: 978-1-4897-3768-7 (sc)
        978-1-4897-3767-0 (hc)
        978-1-4897-3769-4 (e)

Print information available on the last page.

LifeRich Publishing rev. date: 08/31/2021

A soft breeze was blowing this lazy autumn afternoon at the local airport. Milo, a bull terrier dog, was sleeping comfortably in his warm bed when all of a sudden a bright yellow leaf, which had been dancing with the wind, landed gently on his head.

Milo, being Milo, didn't jump up or be afraid. He just opened one sleepy eye, looked up, and seeing that it was just a leaf, went back to his dreams, snoring lightly into his soft red plaid blanket, the leaf staying right where it landed between his furry ears.

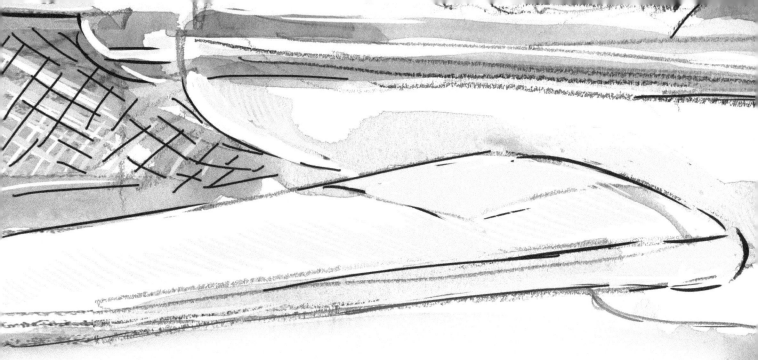

Jack, the pilot, and Milo's best friend, was standing next to his shiny little plane and watched the happy leaf do the dance onto Milo's head. The sight of his silly pup snoozing made him smile and he began to hum a bit as he finished polishing the wing of his airplane.

"That Milo!" He said out loud, interrupting his humming, "Nothing stops him from his naps! I think he's tired out from all that napping!"

Not really wanting to wake his furry friend but knowing they had a mission ahead, Jack walked over, leaned down and brushed the lively leaf off his pup's head, gave his head a soft rub, and then scratched him gently behind one fuzzy ear.

"Okay, my sleepy friend, it's time to go! We have a job to do!"

"We need to take care of some very important business at another airport and I think you're the perfect pup to help me out. Are you ready?"

As soon as Milo felt Jack rub his head and say the words "go" and "job," his nap…and the leaf…were instantly forgotten and he jumped up onto his four sturdy legs, yawned and stretched, and gave Jack a great big doggy smile!

"That's my Milo! Let's go, Buddy; it's time for another adventure!"

Giving Milo one last rub on his ear, Jack started for the hangar and Milo followed eagerly at his heels, his short legs keeping up with Jack's long stride, but he did turn back once to give that discarded leaf a last stern look. He was reminding the leaf of just who was in charge!

"Come on, Milo, get in your seat. I've got to strap you in," Jack said.

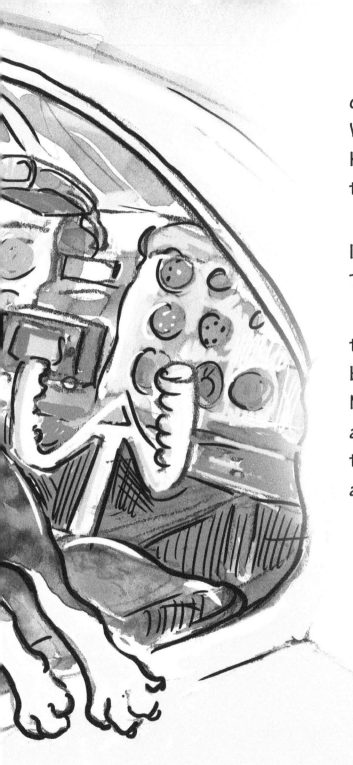

Milo, being a bull terrier dog, was big on bulk but he was not so long in the legs. Without Jack's help, Milo could not jump high enough to reach his seat so Jack had to help him to his chair.

Milo loved to fly with Jack. And Jack loved to have Milo next to him when he flew. They were best friends.

Jack didn't have to explain to Milo where they were going or what they were doing, but Jack always wanted to make sure Milo knew where they were headed off to and what they were going to do, so before take off, Jack would always explain their adventure to Milo.

Jack loved to fly and he loved his plane. It was a doozey! It wasn't brand new and it didn't have all the bells and whistles like a new plane, but his plane was fast and sleek. It was just fine for an old pilot like Jack. He kept it shined and polished all the time, working to keep it in tip top shape so it was ready whenever he and Milo were needed.

Once Jack had helped Milo up into the seat, he strapped him in and put his special doggy headset on so the sounds of the plane wouldn't bother him and so Milo could hear Jack talk while they were flying.

"Okay, Milo," Jack said through the headset, "are you ready to fly a bit north?" Milo turned his head to look at Jack and saw him smile and say, "We're off to pick up a pup that needs a home. I was hoping you would help him feel better about the plane ride." Milo's eyes got wide and bright and he gave Jack a quick but happy bark and settled in his seat. Milo was ready for take-off!

Jack then explained to Milo that they were off to pick up an abandoned dog at another airport and the flight would only take about an hour. Milo stayed very alert and sat up very straight in the seat while Jack read his flight list to check that all the instruments were working. He knew the words that Jack was saying were things that had to be done before they could leave. But then his heart raced and he gave a low woof when Jack yelled "Clear!" which Milo knew was the word that meant they were ready to fly!

Carefully guiding the plane to the runway, Jack was cleared for takeoff by the voice over the radio and Milo's heart skipped a beat! He couldn't wait to be up in the air! Milo loved the take-offs and the landings! His heart would jump up and down in his big broad chest, and it was all he could do to hold in that sharp bark he would do when he was excited.

He had to stay still, though, and quiet or he would make trouble for Jack. First, they would start real slow, but then all of a sudden the little plane zoomed down the runway and Milo could feel the wheels leave the ground. Jack gently guided the plane Up! Up! Up! And just like that, they were flying and Milo could see all the buildings and houses and the tops of trees! He was so happy!

Milo's favorite thing to do was to look out the window as they flew high in the air, watching as the clouds floated past him, with the ground far below.

As they flew, Milo shifted a bit in the seat so he could keep his eye on Jack, just in case his best friend needed him, but Jack was true to his word and the flight was very short. Jack was now preparing the plane for landing. "Okay, Boy, you did great! You're the best co-pilot ever! We're going to put the gear down now and head straight for the runway. I couldn't have done it without you!"

Milo liked it when Jack was happy. "Give me a high five, Boy!" Milo lifted his paw and touched Jack's hand and wriggled a bit back in his seat, getting ready for the landing!

Jack tipped the wings to the side, turning the little plane toward the airport's runway. He put the wheels down and slowed the plane so they could make a safe landing. Milo's eyes were glued to the long white strip painted on the wide road which was coming up fast! Two short bounces and they were down!

Milo was not surprised that Jack landed the plane without any problems. Jack was the best pilot ever! "Okay, Milo, we have to meet George at the opposite end of the airport, so it will be just a few more minutes until we can get out of the plane."

Jack taxied over to park the plane near a hangar at the end of the road. Milo could barely sit still while Jack unstrapped him and took off his headset. Jack lifted Milo out of the seat and helped him to the ground. Once he was back on all four paws, he looked up and blinked at the bright sun and sniffed the air. He then gave a quick bark and did a bully dog twirl! He was so excited! He was ready to meet his new friend!

Once on the ground and out of the plane, Jack and Milo walked over to a hangar at the edge of the airport. There were so many buildings and all of them had different kinds of airplanes in them. There were so many different styles of planes in all kinds of colors! Some planes had high wings, and some planes had low wings. And some planes had four wings! Milo thought airports were so much fun! Just the thing for a smart and happy bully dog!

Jack waved to a man as they came close to a big green hangar. The man waved back at Jack and said something Milo couldn't hear. Jack laughed. Once they reached the big door, the man came out to meet them and shook Jack's hand. "Welcome to my airport, Jack! You too, Milo! I've heard a lot of good things about you!"

Milo was sitting at Jack's feet listening to the two men. Jack looked down and smiled at Milo. He shrugged his shoulders, chuckling a bit. "Milo, you know you're famous! All the pilots know about you."

Milo tilted his head to the side and gave Jack his best don't-fool-me bully look. "Don't worry, Milo, they all love you! You're the best co-pilot around!"

Jack and George laughed and Milo felt better so he gave an I-forgive-you bark and waited to see what Jack and George would do next.

George turned to both of them and said, "Come on in you two! How was the flight? Did you run into any bad weather?"

Milo, being Milo, felt he had to report all the news first. He gave a quick bark and shook his head, settling himself right next to Jack's side.

Jack chuckled at Milo's flight report. "Just like Milo said, George, the flight was great" Jack said. "No wind and a clear sky. It was perfect flying weather!" The two men laughed and spoke for a minute about things Milo didn't understand. Milo wasn't really listening now. He wanted to find this new friend Jack told him about. He had come all this way and he had not seen or smelled a trace of another dog.

Well, Milo didn't like to wait. Milo was here to help. He paced around the hangar for a bit, sniffing and peeking into boxes. He did not see any signs of a new friend. He began to growl and bark, letting Jack and George know he was here to do a job.

"All right, Boy, I know. You're right. We came here to help. Let's see what George has for us."

Milo came back to Jack's side. George went first, walking to the back of the building, with Jack and Milo following them, his short legs keeping up with their long strides. It was darker here and very quiet except for a low whine coming from the corner of the room. Milo heard the noise and stopped suddenly. Sniffing the air, he approached slowly, ears alert, and he saw the reason for the trip.

In the corner of the hangar was a big wire cage. Inside of the cage was a small, scruffy pup with big brown eyes. Milo thought he was the saddest dog he had ever seen. Milo gave a slight whine and looked at Jack, wide-eyed. He gently wagged his tail and nudged Jack's shoe. Milo didn't like this at all! Pushing Jack's shoe with his big nose, Milo wanted Jack to open the cage.

"I know, Boy, I know," Jack quietly said. "This little guy has had it rough. George found him near the fence around the far side of the airport and he didn't have any name tag or a place to go.

George picked him and has had him for a couple of days. He put up Lost and Found signs and called all the people he knows, but so far no one has claimed him. George told me he named him Gizmo. He thought he needed a happy name. He figured that maybe you and I could help him." Milo liked that idea. Milo liked to help everybody.

Milo approached the crate carefully, not wanting to scare Gizmo. Stopping just about a foot away, he leaned in and sniffed. Gizmo, who had been crouched in the back of the crate, lifted his head and sniffed too. Milo gave a low, soft woof and Gizmo slowly came over to Milo and they touched noses. Gizmo took a step back and wagged his tail, Milo's tail started to wag too and then they both did a little happy dance to celebrate a new friend!

Jack and George both burst out laughing. "Okay, Milo," that's enough! You are going to get him all excited and then we can't fly. I can see that you two are now best friends. Let's get Gizmo in the plane and go home." Milo backed away a bit but he couldn't help doing a couple of full twirls and leaps to show Gizmo how happy he was that he was coming with them. Gizmo gave a small, but happy bark and he started to finally wag his tail. He liked Milo!

George opened the door to the cage and Gizmo slowly came out.

He still wasn't sure of what was going to happen to him.

Milo stood by and watched, whining and pacing, giving a helpful woof to Gizmo every few minutes. Jack found a bowl and filled it with water. Milo turned and gave a quick bark at Jack. "Oh, thank you, Milo. I did forget." Reaching into his pilot bag, Jack brought out Milo's special doggy cookies. "Here you go, Gizmo. This is from Milo to you. These are his special cookies and he wants you to have one!" Reaching down, he held it for Gizmo who gave one sniff, looked a Jack, and gently took the cookie from Jack's hand. Munching the treat, Gizmo seemed to feel better about things, his tail wagging gently on the hangar floor.

"Milo," Jack said, "that was just the thing to do! You are the best! George was right to think you would be such a big help! I don't think we could have done this without you!"

Milo liked it when Jack said nice things to him but his job was not done yet. Milo stayed by Gizmo's side until he was done eating and drinking, and then took Gizmo outside for a walk around the hangar. Jack called to them and the two pups trotted back to the hangar, side by side, now fast friends.

Gizmo would have to travel in the crate. He was not used to flying and it was for everyone's safety that Gizmo would be in the cage while flying home.

Gizmo did not want to go back into the cage. Once again, Milo came to the rescue. Milo gently woofed and growled and nudged Gizmo back into the crate, and when Jack shut the door and latched it, Milo put his paw through the wire and touched Gizmo on the head. Gizmo gave a cheerful bark! He was ready to go!

So Jack picked up the crate, carrying it over to the plane and he and George settled Gizmo in the backseat of the plane with a special puppy seat belt. Milo looked on to make sure Gizmo was doing okay and he let out one happy "woof."

When he saw Gizmo's wagging tail, Jack smiled back at his playful pup and said to Milo, "Okay, Milo, let's get going. We want to make sure we have plenty of light to fly home in."

So up into the sky they all went, Jack, Milo and Gizmo, heading back home to find a new forever family for their new friend.

There are more adventures waiting for Jack and Milo and they want you to come along!

Keep track of these two fearless flyers to find out where their next fun flight will take them!

Go to Jack and Milo's website for more information or to purchase another copy of The Adventures of Jack and Milo!

Website: jackandmilo.com

Facebook Page: facebook.com/The-Adventures-of-Jack-and-Milo-101430288142070

Lightning Source UK Ltd.
Milton Keynes UK
UKHW050630130921
390486UK00005B/10